Theodore Mouse GOES TO SEA

by MICHAELA MUNTEAN
ILLUSTRATED BY LUCINDA McQUEEN

A GOLDEN BOOK • NEW YORK
Western Publishing Company, Inc., Racine, Wisconsin 53404

J

Every morning
Theodore Mouse woke up
with the sunrise.

He made his bed.
He brushed his teeth.
He combed his whiskers.

Then he climbed to the roof of his house and looked out over the rooftops of the other mouse houses. He looked out beyond the trees, and beyond the shoreline, to the sea.

"Every morning is the same," Theodore said. "I make my bed. I brush my teeth. I comb my whiskers. Then I climb up to the roof. The only thing that changes," Theodore sighed, "is the sea. Sometimes it is rough and wild, and sometimes it is smooth as glass."

Then Theodore Mouse thought of something he had never thought of before. "I will go to sea!" he cried. "I will sail around the world, and every morning I will wake up in a new and different place."

But then Theodore thought of something else he hadn't thought of before. He didn't have a boat. He sat for a while, wondering what to do.

"My bed will be my boat!" Theodore decided. "My sheet will be my sail, and I will be the captain of my ship!"

So Theodore huffed and puffed and pushed and pulled his bed to the shore.

His mother and father and sisters and brothers and aunts and uncles all came to see him off.

"What if you meet Pirate Cats?" his mother cried.

"I will bash them and smash them!" Theodore answered bravely.

"What if you meet Wild Water Rats?" his sister cried.

"I will bop them and bang them!" Theodore replied. And off he sailed.

Theodore saw many things he had never seen before.

He sailed to warm tropical lands. He ate mangoes and pineapple and slept under palm trees.

He sailed to snowy, icy lands. He met Eskimo mice who taught him how to cut holes in the ice and fish in the cold waters.

Then one day, while Theodore was sailing, a big storm
blew up. The sky turned black. The boat rocked this
way and that. Theodore's stomach rocked this way and
that, too.

Just when he thought things couldn't get any worse, they did.

A big ship of Pirate Cats sailed up on his port side!

A big ship of Wild Water Rats sailed up on his starboard side!

Poor Theodore was all alone in the middle. What was he going to do?

Suddenly Theodore had an idea. He threw one of his
pillows at the cats. He threw his other pillow at the
rats.

Feathers flew in all directions. They stuck to the wet
fur of the Pirate Cats. They stuck to the wet fur of the
Wild Water Rats.

The feathers made them <u>sneeze</u> and
<u>wheeze</u> and cough and <u>gasp</u>. But all
Theodore Mouse did was laugh.

"Ha, ha!" he cried. "You all look like a
bunch of chickens!" And he sailed away
as fast as he could.

The sky cleared. The sun shone. "I think it is time to set sail for home," said Theodore Mouse.

Theodore's mother and father and sisters and brothers and aunts and uncles were all at the shore to meet him. They were happy to see Theodore, and he was very happy to see them.

Everyone helped him push and pull his bed back to his house. As soon as he got there, Theodore fell fast asleep.

The next morning he woke up with the sunrise. He made his bed and brushed his teeth and combed his whiskers.

Then Theodore Mouse climbed to the roof of his house, where all the other mice were waiting to hear about his wonderful adventures on the high seas.